T0193735

WINGAR HOGAN'S
BUSH
SAFARI

The Big Bush Gang Adventure at Bunyip

JAMES JONES

BALBOA.
PRESS
A DIVISION OF HAY HOUSE

Balboa Press books may be ordered through booksellers or by contacting:

Balboa Press
A Division of Hay House
1663 Liberty Drive
Bloomington, IN 47403
www.balboapress.com.au
1 (877) 407-4847

Print information available on the last page.

ISBN: 978-1-5043-0367-5 (sc)
ISBN: 978-1-5043-0368-2 (e)

Balboa Press rev. date: 07/27/2016

ingar hogans bush safari..by author james jones 2nd june 2015 chapter 1.the italian job. Part one Wingar and his crew take 20 eyeties for a cultural tour up north to broome,across to darwin and to,alice and down the gunbarrel highway to kalgoolie,then back to perth..part 2 the true blue world tour part 3 bunger mackenzie the sperm whale whisperer.--.two ww2 veterans were sittin out,front on the porch of dan drongo,s pub at enebba in west aussie,sippin ice cooled cans of vb beer.bingo the kelpie pup who was under the table,heard a sound in the distance,he stood up and with ear,s pricked,and growled.tom hicks said,bingo is onto somthin dan,his hearin is 300 times better

than us mate,and he can see for 10 miles clear as a bell.jesus bugger me,never knew that tom.said dan. then dan saw a huge italian flag movin above the tree,s,five miles away and grabbed the telescope,his grandpa given him.dan had a good long look and said,we are being invaded by the eyetie army tom,4 bloody army trucks and six h.j holden panel vans. there is some big bastard,on the top mount of the cabin,bangin away with sniper rifle,a 303 i reckon and there is 3 dead roo,s tied to the side of the first truck,bloody hell is this another mad max movie crowd .tom started laughin,and bingo barked like hell.sit down bingo and,now dan its bloody wingar hogan and his grand safari mob.you know them and remember what happened the last time they came thru here.said tom. dan thought for a while,and smiled.aah yeah,the german baker bloke who was stung by a swarm of vicious wild bees,when he lit a camp fire under there hive in the tree they called home,what a wacker.that caper really pissed the bees,right off.15 minutes later the army convoy arrived,with a fat italian colonel in uniform standing in the cab of the first truck,with a 303 rifle and,waving his country,s flag,shouting viva italia,da best a vino,da best a women and da best a pasta.then the vehicles drove in and lined up at the service station for petrol and lpg gas.tom said,i listen to my mates in perth on my c.b.radio and tune in to see what the wingar safari mob is up too. yesterday arvo,i heard 4 eyetie blokes demanding akubra hats,cheese, 10 types of salami and a secret supply of grappa,without the shelia,s knowin of course.a right sneaky bloke,he gave em 4 first aid kits,with extra large,thermos flasks full of the good stuff.he also told sam to put a 50 gallon keg of grappa in the freezer van, marked olive oil for cookin see,for later on.mario salina,vincenti alma and colonel diaz came to drongo,s pub for a counter lunch.tom hicks was wearing his father,s 4th light brigade slouch hat with an emu feather stuck in the side,which colonel diaz recognised immediatly. He walked up,snapped his heels and saluted to tom and dan.bloody hell he is goin to declare war thought,dan senor it is how you say da utmosta privillage to meet a officer of the famous light horse brigado .a barman stepped out of the pub,with 3 chairs,and a barmaid followed with plates of canapes,chips cheese and nuts.tom and dan stood up and shook hands with the 3 italians.tom said colonel this is my father,s hat,he was in the charge at beersheba when they wiped out the arabs .the gutless pommy generals were total cowards from the first day of world war one .the poofter general allenby the worst piece of shit,a coward in and must be court martialed,the book beersheba prove all detials hidden records from 1200 bc to 2015 to protect all forms of footpad,s pickpocket,s shonky slimey officers, barrister con men whose law.s are a con job from 1600 and do not use common law,and breaks all constition laws, a total cover up from 1880 from the lords of scum and slave labour,who exist now the british army 7 charges loosing 1000s of men .they are all mass muderer,s like mussalini,you understand not me.i served in sicily and and in france from d,day onwards, me and dan were comando,s secret jobs behind enemy lines,to sabotage and raid every where,comprendo mate.si i understand,and show great respect for your father tomiso.now i buy you dinner si..later they all went inside for a big counter lunch,cooked by salina a retired italian chef,called on by dan drongo when needed.an excellent meal was enjoyed by all,in the lounge that night.the dead roo,s were cut up,and chucked in the freezer. at 2,40 am there was a howling screech,from some where under ground.rosita and sophia rushed out of there tent,with torches to investigate the source of the sound.more howling came from the south,even louder this time.rosita saw a bore hole,and raced towards it.she shone her led torch down.mumma mia sophia,look at dat said rosita,there was aldo manilla,the huge fat mayor,from palermo,drunk as a skunk a on grappa 100% proof. He was chest a deep in a mud,rosita even claimed she smell da pigga s breath from the top of a the well .a very pissed drover waco tomson.strolled over from his toyota,ute,and chucked an oxen,s yoke down the well,yellin for the eyetie, to put it around his neck,and i,ll pull ya up mate with me winch cable, piece of piss,waco tomson said the yoke knocked out aldo,when the yoke struck his head. .sgt bronson arrived fast,in a navara,with blue lights flashing,and seachlights blazing. the whole camp site,was woken up,and came towards the well.wingar get a truck over here fast,mate your high falutin mayor is up shit creek and might drown in the bore.said sgt bronson .sam tilson went down the bore hole,on the 10 ton winch run off the mercedez unimog,and tied a halter around aldo.up he went in 20minutes,and he was on dry land, and taken to the shower,s.sam tilson came up much later,after he called wingar on his mobile.he had found an old steel chest wrapped in oilcloth.sgt bronson arrested the dropkick drover,waco tomson and headed back to the police station.all the crowd were,ordered back to bed.after a wash,a set of bolt cutter.s,to snap the lock,sam.s box was opened to reveal .1 a map for lassiters reef,location,in the desert near lake cristopher,230 small natural gold nuggets and 12 pieces of fine quality jade,and a log book of mining claims from 1790.by a man known as james van der veen,barrister at law,captian of vessel retribution, he had recorded sites where his crew,had landed at 12 places on west coast australis,with longtitude and latitudes.well fuck my brown dog,get the scales out sam,said wingar hogan,we have to weigh the lot.$750000 worth of gold,and 1,million worth of ancient provenance marked jade was,the total value of gold .the jade in the open market would fetch unlimited prices at auction.the jade was ming dynasty,purchased by the captian in 1780 in shanghai,on a voyage to pick up a cargo of opium .not a word to anyone sam about this find okay.we will have to check,these mining claims and find a way to sell the loot.said wingar.then he went to check,on the 4,200 gallon tanks of canabis oil specially fitted on the unimog trucks.after a very late start,and a full mechanical check,on all vehilcles the mad wingar convoy headed north,to the overlander roadhouse.all the girls were dead keen,to enjoy the a boat trip where you see the dolphins swimming underwater and all other sea life,as well. the italian men,went fishing or went with sam tilson. to the high tourist lookouts to take photos and make rough sketches for painting,s to be completed later.wingar hogan,was doing some paper work on his shonky tax paper.s when his mobile phone rang. Bill dickson the skipper of the game fishing,charter boat swordfish,said the italians have caught a marlin,and 35 large barramundi,now the idiots,want to catch a 40 foot white pointer shark,they saw.did you know there is a american film crew,here making the jaws 5 film. colonel diaz,and his two mates offered me 5 grand to chase.the bigga ceaser,the emporer of all shark.s.well go for it bill,sam picket the film director is a friend of my dad.i will call him,and let him know .he can film you blokes in action,and it is good,advertising for my safari outfit.you can find a real white pointer later,okay bill said to wingar. sam picket got his film crew,and producer organised from 2 boat and a chopper to give the italian,s a few chances to catch big bertha,the mechanical white pointer.his screenwriter was,already adding more scene,s to the film.mario salina. was on the deck of swordfish,searching all around,with field glasses for bigga ceaser.vincenti helped colonel daiz strap up,in the game fishing chair and handed him a huge rod with a10000 pound breaking strain fishing line attached.the,re she blow,s on the port bow be bloody twice the size of moby dick,that

huge bloody white whale,bugger me,shouted bill
smiling widely.where is a bloody .port a bow billy
said mario.off to your left,and starboard is on the
right side of this boat okay mate said bill.mario
looked to port,and shouted. Dio mio,A big a shark
fin twenty feet a tall,colonel mumma mia the
emperor for sure.the supposed shark dived under
the surface,then ten minutes later the sperm whale
sprung up.into the air and flopped on it,s side.false
alarm colonel but,there is another wopper, fish
astern said bill.just after a crewman,attached a
safety harness for the colonel,his fishing rod,was
nearly ripped from his strong grip,with both hands.
the line went taught,and swung to the left.vincenti
grabbed the colonel,from behind,worried he might
be pulled right off the fuckin game fishing chair.
bill came down,with a ratchet and tightened the
mounting bolts into the deck.mario saw big bertha,s
huge body,come to the surface,and submerge and
said.he is a huge giant killer,and might attack our
boat be careful colonel.said mario.i have la
emperor,he will not escape me,mario.yelled the
colonel.vincenti get a my a bloody ventilla

shotgun,and a bigga spear guns.we blast him to a hella and a gone,when i get him alongside hokay. the emperor swung to the right,and came near the side the boat.vincenti,aimed and fired seven shots,into the head and body of the shark and mario let go with 8 shots from the 4 shot gun loaded spear guns on deck.bill and his two,crew men were laughing there heads off,watching these crazy eyeties.big bertha circled the swordfish and broke,the fishing line connected to the colonel,s rod.mario took more shots at the shark when it came close,then it vanished.the big bloody bastardo where did it go billy.said mario.gone real deep mate,and might be dying from all them,shotgun wounds.the other shark,s will attack and eat it,when they smell the blood. Three decent size sharks were caught later,and the swordfish sailed back to port. sam picket the director phoned wingar,to say he got a good two hours of film from bill,s on board camera,s, of crazy eyeties doin there stuff on jaws 5 the mechanical shark.take some video,s,as your drive around on ya safari mate,and i will add those to the movie ok mate.i have two with me,sam ill send them over by courier.said winger.a delay of four days,was needed,before aldo the mayor was released from the bush hospital.wingar,s convoy arrived at cararvon three days later,without incident. sam then took 9 eyeties down the mooka,river to go gold prospecting,and check wally jumbuck.s old gold mine,where 50000 tons of gold had been foundover the last 60year,s.many said there was a million tons left,at least .metal detectors and pans were,used in the river with four men getting 5 nuggets between them.giuseppi talva found a large quatrz reef,and he chipped away with his miner.s hammer.he saw patches of gold,and asked don tosmo to sweep his detector over the da spot.the detector set off a very loud signal.the don grabbed a small shovel, and dug a hole 2 feet deep and 1 foot across.giuseppi picked up a handfull of gold pieces,and shouted da big a strike,a don tosmo.sam strolled up,and washed the gold in a pan.the he said sorry mate fools gold,it is found in mica in strata,s of quartz,which you have here.keep digging on the signal,ok lads.mario came to help his mates,and after making a huge hole 5 feet across and four foot deep,a milk churn and a ship,s anchor was found. when the milk churn was,upended 6 old note books and 132 coins in, small tobacco tins.florins.french spanish,and dutch coins of different value was found,..sam tilson checked,the detector the don, was using,and made some adjustments.your discriminators were not set right don.you and the boys could have dug up twenty of tons of useless steel, ha ha,he said.rino and benni had checked a turn in the river,for any quartz bearing rocks.benni slammed his pick into a mound of sand,and sat down on a flat rock,in the shade of a coolibah tree nearby to light his pipe.rino was poking around in a hole,on the side of the mooka river.a six foot tree python slithered down,the tree trunk to check benni out as a meal for the day.the light brown python slid up close and sniffed benni out,just as15 large bull ants bit him on both legs.benni saw the snake,and opened his mouth in shock,dropping his lit pipe into his crutch.hot ashes set his bush clothes on fire,and he believed the snake had bitten him a dozen times at least.get a bloody water and a doctorio rino, a huge anconda bite a me all over.he screamed,rino looked up.from his work site,when a fourteen foot goanna disturbed by all the din,shot out close by rino and ran down his back,under benni,s legs and on down the river then stopped,cocked his left leg for a long piss.dat a was a bloody huge a dragon rino,you scared da shit out of him,and he attack me. stupido,now get da fuckin water quick. The don arrived in a rush and emptied 2 buckets of water on benni,then he saw 1000s of bull ants storming all over there large nest,where benni had smashed his hammer into the ground. like a wingar say benni,you are a first a class a wanker .next thing you try to kill a kangaroo with your mining hammer rino and a the don stripped benni.s pants of and threw him,in the river to wash away the bull ants.two more eyeties were bitten by wasp,s when they dislodged a nest.after the sun went down sam got a barby goin,and laid on a shower,and cold beer,s for all,sam slipped three of the nuggets he found,into the bucket,s of soil the eyeties were washing.these big finds made the mining trip a huge success,and would be talked about for years to come.the size and number of nuggets found would increase,with the telling of the story by each famous eyeti miner.the italian ladies meanwhile,had been scuba diving,and attended art classes at a local winery.a two week period was spent at carnarvon,then off north the convoy went again.a week of rest at broome,and a good time for all repair,s to the convoy vehicles.at banjo.s creek hideaway,the tourist,s went on there first camel ride,along the beach.the colonel spent up big,and conned his fellow italian,s into wearing fancy arab robes like lawrence of arabia.he even arranged to import two,racing camels home to sardinia.rosa was at the rear of the camel,train when a cheeky dingo ran in close,barking furiouslyand biting the camels legs, making her camel bolt.sam rode along side on his horse,and plucked her off the wild beast just in time.two days later colonel diaz and 4 mates,were reading tourist brochures.they had met lord lipton at the raffles hotel bar.you come all the way by yacht from england to buy a plane si.said the colonel .very true but this aircraft is rare,and has been fully restored and only 3 are left in the world. A 200 horse power gypsy moth,in canary yellow colour..my son has a spitfire in a hangar, at my estate in kent.a spot to fast for me colonel.shall we have a picnic lunch,at chips flying circus airstrip tomorrow gents when my plane arrives,said his lordship.si we look at da moth yes and many other planes,i will arrange the food and wine hokay lord a.said colonel diaz. spiffing show,old chap said lord lipton.the italian ladies went,on a cruise to the local gorges by ferry,and all the men were up early.the colonel and mario had bought flying leather jackets,silk scarves and goggles also biggles leather capsfrom 2 local ex fighter pilots for $900 each outfit,to look da part. wingar had the canteen truck along,and led the men to the airstrip.lord lipton had picked up,mario and the colonel before hand in his vintage car,and were sipping scotch now from the inbuilt bar in the 1936 rolls royce la gonda .as the roller drove along the side of the circus paddock a p51 mustang came thundering in above the car with 20 feet to spare. the mustang flew thru the open large door,s of a large hangar,then strait up to 2000ft did a victory roll and a loop the loop,then landed to refuel.i say a veteran without doubt,damn good flying what. said his lordship.bloody hell,my heart she flutter,s,a hot sweat a said mario.well old boy,if your shit scared now,on the ground,with a passing rumble like that you will never have what it takes to be a pilot .said lord lipton.wingar pulled up beside the control tower,with the panel vans and the roller did a tour of the hangars where all 10 aircraft were stored.chips dundee,s flying circus had 6 tiger moths,a spitfire,a mustang a sabre jet and a areo wing areobatic plane.10 mechanics and 20 pilots on shifts. During the wet or slack times,charter flights,mail and freight services were always busy.a 2 day arranged visit was extended to 4weeks due to very keen interest by all the italians on site.a bright yellow gypsy moth flew in one hour after wingars mob arrived.the pilot even,had a helmet and flying jacket on,in the same colour as the plane. Mumma mia a mona lisa,plane a true work of a art a micheal angelo he could a make dis,for sure,said mario,when he saw it.magnifico a master craftsman a didda a perfecto restorio si said the colonel.the pilot got down from the plane,and walked towards them,taking off the yellow helmet.maria loren was,an italian air force capitano,on leave.you are a lord lipitoni si,and saluted .here are all the casa papers log book ecetera .she said and handed them to the driver of the roller.i am maria,sophia loren,s daughter senor,an capitano in the italiono airforce. my brother renae restored the,the english yellow rose.james van der veen the sign writer,has painted the name on each side of the fuselarge,and on the sides of the tail wing in gold leaf,with a black border.four coats of clear,also were applied later, She said.good gacious me a lady ace,in my english rose,absolutley perfect my dear,may i offer you champagne and canapes after your long tiring flight from bungowannah,in nsw.wingar and his crew set up tents,tables and drinks in iced buckets and eskies.mario asked maria,about the aviation company,that restored the gypsy moth.bunn brothers aviation,they are world famous and the quality of there craft,has no equal in australia.after a long 3 hour lunch,chips dundee joined them for a coffee,and said colonel like to take a test flight in my spit,we just fitted a new engine in her.senor it would truly be,an honour,to fly widda air marshal chippa dundee si i.accept.good and get ya self a pair of flying boots pilot officer diaz its gets bloody cold at 1000 feet,said chips.sam tilson said lord lipton my cousin harry flynn taught me to fly,in a gypsy moth ten years ago,and i have a 200hp job in perth. can i take you up for 20 minutes.very good and please instruct me,as we fly .i only have 30 hours training time,sam,said lord lipton.off the two men went to the gypsy english rose,got aboard and sam took off,after his lordship spun the prop and a full warm up and check was made of the plane first. both aircraft went out to the coast and along the beach,then chips flew at different heights,making adjustments to controls for best performance.he tested flaps and all mechanical parts.which the colonel recorded for him in a casa logbook.on the way back to the circus air strip,chips went thru a set of manouvers to test the airframe.he saw the english rose 4000ft below,and smiled.3 miles from the strip,sam was at 60knots,when he heard a shout from lord lipton on his radio.upstairs sam old bean,we have company.the spitfire was upside down,60 feet above them coming in at 60knots to keep position.sam adjusted his speed to suit,until he came in,and touched down.the spitfire rolled level and came in over the control tower,dropping a small parachute with a parcel attached,which landed next to maria loren.she ran out,and opened the parcel attached to the chute.a message was insdie,which read .to a lady mistress of the sky,a black pearl for each capitano,s bar .from chips and your brother possum .the parcel contained a velevet box,with a platinum necklace with 2 one inch pearls and a matching ring with a small pearls. chips dundee came around in a circle and landed,then taxied the spit to the hangar.her name,was p.o. bader .the restored original plane the fighter acc flew in 243 squadron from kent.pilotta officer daiz,had to be helped from the cockpit,by 3 of his mates.3hours earlier on,banjo patterson editor of the broome bugle,got a call from tom hicks at enebba.wingar.s at the circus strip now,the usual fee ok banjo,toms brother was working in the broome control tower.jesus christ,lord lipton is here,and 10 italians from the mafia gang in sicily,the daiz,bloke is the godfather,the don .said banjo.4 reporters had driven at 150kph to the airstrip and used camera,video,s and even hired a cherry picker to film and record all the action.a display would be on,in one week for 40,000 people,and 300 aircraft and glider.s would fly in.p.o.daiz took 2 days and a massage and herbal bath to recover from the aerobatic effects of his flight.many phone calls to italy were made by 4 italian men, to sotheby,s auction house and real estate agents.mario,benni and the colonel formed a flying tourist company called true blue sky.s there base would be in naples at mario,s old italian air force base . Six properties were sold in rome and tuscany,with all the activity going banjo the editor at the broome bugle got a phone call,at his local coffee shop.bazza turnbull,was a an expert and a telstra technicain,hacker top class. he informed banjo $25 million had been transfered from mafia accounts in sardinia,sicily and italy.the bastards are screaming there arse off in italian,and god knows what other lingo,the 3 guys ya put me onto are all related to the 4 top mafia famlies.no trace of drugs or tax evasion were found,and colonel diaz is the pope,s cousin,so be careful banjo.said bazza.another reporter sent a message stating mario salina owned 2 tuscany winery,s in share deals with the garaboldi family.thank,s bazza keep the hot tips, comin mate and check up on all the italian blokes and women .ok.chips dundee was asked about,a range of aircracft for sale in australia and which companies sold the best restored planes.he gave them a few magazines,business cards and internet addresses to research,then got on the phone to organise his big air show.there would be,1 bombing runs.areobatics,formation flying with multi coloured smoke flowing from the wings.a man or woman strapped to the top of each tiger moth plane as they flew around the strip.parachute drops,with fake piglets,chooks and dummy kangaroo.s and dummy politicans,s with suit,s and blue ties like the drongo abbot and full of fresh bullshit,and full of water melon,to burst on impact. kids games and races.wing walking the lot.25 top pilots were coming to fly,and enjoy the fine show .the mad max car crew drove in with mel gibson and tina turner with all there wild cars from the filming site 10 miles away.dame edna,had several show,s lined up,and the top australian political and finance society and political advisor sir les patterson flew in with dame edna on a pink plane,with huge rose clourued sunglasses 5o feet wide mounted on the top wing,s of a herculees air force 2ⁿᵈ hand job.free travel of course as a dame.100s of cars and vans arrived 5000 miners flew in, instead of going home on leave,3000 more tradesmen than needed had came to do nothing but watch.but jesus who was watching,the watcher,s frank snowden a dark underground hacker sent an encrypted message via bazza to banjo.patterson bazza said,$700million changed hands to a bloody dutch tulip factory,then a chicago gambino mob,got the receipt,and get this the top 4 mafia guys will be at broome tomorrow,they use a bloody code word which is always orange,what the fuck does that mean.a bloody citrus fruit code .there is 100s of types of bank accounts etc.a e mail arrived at the bugle office to say tina turner has,just arrived to give a concert,and the mad max movie director is,sending all the vehicles to the air circus show.a new movie around broome in 2 months will be filmed called ABBOTS TRAIN WRECK, about a group of lnp pollies,4 priests and 2 cardinals attacked on a trip to beagle bay .the gang are a ruthless bunch of lady bikers and cwa women in huge modified john deere tractors and mack trucks.,they are held for ransom of $25.million,and a 100% equality treaty for women to last 1000yrs. the gals blow the rail tracks,drug the food on the train blinfold all the men,and whip them off to cockatoo island in a digiused customs boat.they create a false trail with some old ford utes to dampier downs,underground gold mine,then go up the gegally river by native canoe.s,with help from local aborigine bush tucker gals who know the bush,better even than there hubbies.anything to give a wara ninga wungoona poison words of the cane toad man,meaning a pure a bloody hard time was agreed to asap.the rollin stones,willie nelson,beyonce, kenny rogers and 10 more famous entertainer,s flew in to perform.many for free,and just be there for all the fun.chipps had set up 2 circus shows,now orders came for a film of the shows,and later 4 more with 10 barnstormers joining in with there own aircraft.8 huge blimp,s flew in,with t.v and film crew,s aboard.fourteen b doubles arrived with marquee,s,and catering supplies,before 24 overseas chefs came with tons of exotic wines,sauces and food. John goti a mafia top a don hired a us air force giant transport plane to fly in 8 authentic baron von richthoffen restored circus byplanes from a german museum.he donated 20mill to the german restoration company.who had fixed the planes .25 actors who spoke german were needed at once.then clint eastwood and russell crowe arrived on horseback to do a movie deal with chips dundee.colonel diaz wanted 10%,lord lipton 20%,when tina tuner roared into camp in a gold painted mack truck mobile home,demanding 15% of the movie .clint said flying is about,bravery bullshit and cunning.tina suggested the title, knights of the blue.the 2 directors agreed,as she wanted them to do a movie for her later.the don sent his lawyer,with a cheque for $30mill for 20% of the movie.sir micheal caine arrived with douglas bader,son a raf squadron leader, norm to act and advise on the film set.a blue supermarine mark v spitfire came in at 52 feet,just above the erected marquee,s at 400mph,turned upside down,then went into a full loop to roll upright and land,with blue,white and red smoke jets flowing from the wing tips and center undercarriaige.lord lipton and colonel diaz waved flags as they,stood in the roller,when it drove across the airstrip flat out to meet the spitfire,as it stopped.his lordship,s valet offered cool wet scented towel,s,cigar,s and large ice cooled pewter mugs,of single malt irish whisky to norm and sir micheal.after returning to a private luxury caravan,colonel diaz was informing the 2 poms of the events,which had occured so far,on his bigga busha safari.each story was totally exagerated. The la emperor shark was now 65 feet long and 24 shots were taken at the head and chest of the huge killer,also big billy had rammed da shark twice,with the game boat.lord lipton was quietly reading a detailed synopsis of a book sir micheal had discussed with him earlier.the title was diamonds daimlers and derby winners,a very interesting storyline about smuggling diamonds in cars and horse floats,from the u.k to holland.dutch cheeses,french brandy and other lucritive items were smuggled back on the return trip to england..norm bader excused himself saying,he wanted to see chips dundee and have a look at his father,s spit.the colonel also left,to contact his bank for funds,to pay for his 10% share of the movie.lord lipton said to sir micheal,this book brings back many memories for me,as i was a commando myself in ww2,then did a few year,s in the custom,s service chasing smuggler,s of all kinds.a movie in the great gatsby style would be,an excellent idea .bring in some talented actresses like nicole kidman jennifer lopez,and so on. We need two genuine aussie,chaps for norm and slim brennan,and you could join the cast as the ex mi5 chap what .right up your sleeve old boy.sir micheal said,i agree,and the author has written a second part to this book titled diamonds boats and revenge,later even two movies could be made with a good line up of male characters,half englishand half aussie,s to suit the numbers of ex s,a,s.lads.as your rather busy,at present i shall make a few lists of the actors we need,the backers i can rely on and a short list of directors and producers. said lord lipton.very good,thank you for your genuine interest in my diamond movie .now i shall see what these wild colonial chaps have organised for me,sir micheal said and strolled away.a fine well played steel guitar,could be heard as,willie nelson warmed up for his show.then the real gutsy twang of a top blues man,a doin his thang,was heard. willie looked around and said well damn if it aint ol b. b. King.you gonna have ta play second fiddle this time boy,these bush boys like country more than they dig da blues mr king.well now willie,tina turner just might blow ya clean of the stage boy,then i be takin over,and really get da joint a howling and a screamin to da best new orleans blues.okay b.b your older than me,and need a good nights sleep,so your on after tina.and we both may be outdone by the saphires 4 top local native gals,willie said.in the hangar where the circus planes were parked,8 men sat around on deck chairs.chipps dundee said to sam tilson,how did this boss of your,s get the name wingar sam.well there are several versions,ive heard the truth is young wally hogan aged 12,was at a farm at margret river down south.baldy willows a ww2 ex sniper was using his silenced wetherby 22 rifle,to shoot rabbits nearby.baldy lined up a fat bunny,but it took off as he fired the shot.the bullet hit the side of wally,s left cheek and took a bit of his lower ear off.then went through a bird cage,taking the yellow crest off fred astiare the vicar,s wife pure bred royal cockatoo.fred had been imported from windsor aviary in england.next the bullet hit the church bell causing the fire brigade and ses to be called out,as this was there alarm signal.the bullet bouncing back downtown a large rose was clipped off lady chatterly,s summer hat,as she sipped pinon waar fine red wine from a gold goblet.then the bullet hit the wall of the dorchester hotel,and dropped down into a tequila champgne sunrise cocktail glass,of sophia loren,she was with 6 other famous women movie stars,enjoying a superb french seafood dish on the shaded front porch.sophia in shear terror,threw the glass in the air,and romano the waiter,caught it without spilling a drop of the cocktail.5 police cars arrived after 28 phone calls about shots fired by mad dog morgan,a well known local mentally deranged criminal.he had been caught 4 times on camera pinching flower,s for his mum,and pet chooks and hamsters from the local kindergaten.a star wars palstic ray gun,he always carried in a knitted pack on his back.4 detectives had flown in from perth to catch the crazy maniac,now reputed to have grenades, an rpg and 3 kashikov machine guns.how else could,so many targets be hit at nearly the same time. mean while baldy had hidden his 22 rifle, by tying it in the roof of his feret coop with fencing wire.then baldy took off,flat strap in his holden panel van, for his mine at kalgoolie,and changed his name by deedpole.malcom morgan the supposed,notorious killer was in bali surfing,with his brother,barrister and supreme court judge henry morgan s.c.a 2 week investigation found a phantom,the ghost who prowls the bush caused one shot only to be fired. name unknown a swift silent bullet by misadventure a true mystery to this day said judge rumpold .malcom was never interviewed,the cops were too scared to try it .forensic,checks found all the victims and damage incurred by this ruthless killer .so marget river,hit the world headlines for a week,thats wingars yarn,gentlemen said sam tilson.jesus what a bloody good story,a typical tall tale in true aussie style,and this one is fair dinkum said russell crowe. perty good shootin,reminds me of a few dollars more,when i had to shoot,that greasy mexican off a cross .eli wallach he pissed his pants for real you know said clint eastwood. I shall write a book on these bush character,s,totally outrageous humour,quite halarious said lord lipton.later they all went to dinner and then attend the four hour concert.six spotlights lit up the stage,as the 30piece band started the smash hit simply the best.tina strolled out,real cool like in a blue and white sequaned dress with a short skirt to show off her superb figure.she sang 5 more songs,and the crowd went wild.b.b.king was next,the rolling stones,willie nelson and kenny rogers.then tina turner and the saphires came out as a group.all the gals wore bright red silk dresses.jessica mauboy stood beside tina,with the 3 back up gals shari,miranda and deborah close behind.dock of the bay,was the first song,by otis redding to warm up the audience.2

chuck berry songs,a jerry lee lewis song and nut bush city limits sent the crowd into a wild frenzy. the mad max crew let go with flame thrower.s yelled and screamed in time to the beat.all the crowd was,dancing clapping hands and stomping there feet.instead of 10 songs,the gals had a half hour break and b.b.king played bob dylan,and muddy waters songs.the girls came back on,and tina said she would do an album with the saphires. then they sang 15 more songs,to the delight of the crowd .the whole concert had been filmed,and was a smash hit at the box office later.six concerts were staged,an hour after the end of each air circus show for the crowds to enjoy dinner.james van der veen had cruised around in his white 25 feet holden hurse and,made a range of signs for all the byplanes in the huge dogfight to come on the fisrt day show. raf and raaf roundels .the baron richthoffen royal coat of arms on each side of his fokker,with small panes,painted as the number of kills.on a fine cloudless day at 9am the crowd of 60000 waited,in hushed anticipation,then 6 tiger moths the yellow english rose and a camel,came in at 30feet in vee formation,trailing white whispers of smoke from there wing tips.then they split in different directions to fly in full circles and come back along the airstrip from the opposite direction.behind them and above,came 8 german fokker,s the barons circus,with red smoke coming from there wing tips.camera,s flashed and the huge crowd cheered loudly.all the planes climbed to 4000feet,then a lone brit plane dropped into sight from a cloud and weaved from side to side looking for a enemy target.3 german fokkers appeared up above the brit,to protect there c.o.,then the sneaky baron came up fast from below and behind the brit plane, firing twin schmiesser machine guns that riddled the under belly of the tiger moth.2 puffs of blue smoke came from the moth,and it dived down to weave between some trees.the baron followed,but the brit had swung to port turned and did an emmelman turn got above the baron,gave him a long burst of fire and dropped 2 grenades on his fokker.one grenade bounced off his wing and exploded,and the other missed his cockpit,the baron did an emmelman turn,and fired at the brit again.more smoke from the brit and he flew low around the hanger and landed.2 german planes were shot down in a dog fight above,as the baron with 3 fokkers flew up to assist.3 tiger moths went down,the 2 more as the german fokkers were faster and had better guns.also four or more,to one was there tactics,not one on one attacks is what the kruats used.3 tigers charged at the barons plane,and forced him to go low,and 5 british and aussie machine guns opened up on him.several bullets hit his plane and he weaved all over the sky and landed slumped forward over the controls.then the rest landed the first half was over.next came games for the kids in the break,and after 3 tiger.s flew past 4 times,with 3 girls in black and white flying suits and long scarves,one standing on the top wing in the centre on the petrol tank,between the wings the other 2 on the outsides of each wing.below and between the were 2 small boys hanging on to the uprights.beside each boy was an albino kangaroo 3 feet tall.they came in,and landed as the other 3 tigers came in low with 2 baboons at the ends,of the top wing,each holding the end of a strong rope. on the rope were 6 pink galahs 6 white cockatoo,s and a peregrin falcon,in the middle.the baboon,s were smoking cuban cigar,s too,there favourite brand.real style these darwin bab,s had thought sam tilson the pilot,as he watched them do there stuff above.just shows ya,what an akubara hat,full of grappa,will do for dutch baboon courage.ripper job.the baboons even did a summersalt twice,while still holding the rope,and the birds skwarked to show there appreciation at such acrobatic talent.the german planes did all the manouvers used in action in the air during ww1for an hour.then using real bullets,they came in to straff a line of dummies dressed as hitler,mussalini and abbots whole cabinet look alikes in suits and blue ties.the roullets team arrived next to finish the show,with a top class display.that night lady gaga,beyonce,u2 and madonna were on stage after a large bbq of full steers,camels,crocodiles rabbits and goanna,s on spits.salads fresh seafood truffles,snails frogs legs and many more delicasies were enjoyed being flown in from perth.mario,benni and the colonel stayed on,in broome to finalise all there new business deals.the rest of wingar,s convoy packed,and headed for darwin,via wyndam .at the ord river nature reserve,wingars tourists had stopped to camp for a week.all was calm and quiet,until 2.30.pm when dalina opened one eye.she had been having her usual siesta from noon to 4pm,when she heard a slight ripping sound.chainsaw at 65 foot,was the local rouge salty croc,and was up to his old tricks again.he had chewed 2 guy ropes away from the tent and,had a sniff of dalina and wanted her for a snack,some time this weekafter her body had become decayed.his jaws clamped onto a corner of the tent and the croc crept backwards towards the river 20 feet away.dalina was wide awake now and peeped outside,and screamed like a wild banshee,and then she let off an emergency air horn,she had always at her side.all the local koala,s,put there paws,over there ears,the dogs started howling,and 1000s of birds took flight 6 kelpie dogs from wangabbi station jumped down from there nissan ute,and ran in ta round up the snappin bull croc.wingar dropped his cold,can of vb beer.a fuckin possum has got under the bonnet of my h.j and short circuted my bloody triple claxon,ahoogah horns he said and grabbed a large bag.inside was a rpg,a shotgun 6 grenades and an 1890 sharpes.5o calbre long barrel rifle.sam picked up his steyer machine pistol,and a small flame thrower,off they went to dalina gamboli tent and stopped dead in there tracks.sam said,its the mongrel giant croc chainsaw,wingar see the bright blue tag locked into his neck by albert nama jura the artist and ranger manager last year.fuck this and the kelpies,are goin ape shit too.wingar went forward with the shotgun,fired and blew half of the crocs left front leg off,then tripped over a mangrove root,chainsaw dropped the tent ropes and charged wingar who was flat on the ground.sam cocked his machine gun and aimed to fire,when dalina,s pet 600pound russian wolfhound stalin,pounced on chainsaw and bit his right eye clean out,sam tilson walked strait up,and emptied two 30 round magazines into chainsaw.the croc increased speed fucking roaring angry,and snapped his jaws on contessa lamborgini legs,who had rushed out of her mobile truck to see the commotion this distraction gave wingar the chance to drag out the loaded 50 calbre sharpes rifle and wingar took his famous bisley shootin position and fired.the poisoned high powered bullet,entered the crocs right eye,went thru the brain,and all the way down and out of the tail of chainsaw. .one koala graham kennedy in a nearby tree

Said to paul hogan his treetop flate mate,every time this wanker,wingar,comes rollin thru,it,s real life mate.this desperate housewifes shit is made by pyscholigist mate.and is bullshit. 98% of tv and movies art etc usa shit,puttin all us koala union blokes in the kmcefu members out of business and wreckin the tourist trade.bloody oath,said paul.the kelpic pups were ripping strips off the hide of chainsaw.then steven spellberg flew in with petcr weir,in four white ex blachwarks chopper.cnn had reported falsely reported 30 men and 1 dog 2 canaries 5women and a pet anaconda had been,killed by a huge croc known as mr crusher bloody chainsaw .fuck me the screenplay of this bastard is bigger than jaws 5,that sam picket is doing,for sure said pcter weir .jesus get the whole crew,here and set up the cameras.stephen spellberg said .that night at the movie company camp site,there was heated discussions,about good idea,s for a story line for the film.maria pirelli the make up artist said .you first need to research the history of the big crocodilla this mr chainsaw to see,what the beast has done from a babino.talk to the local tribal elders and native women they know about all the animals and the land.very good maria and we will have to interview all the tourists involved in this horrific attack by this monster said peter weir. geoff wilson a special effects expert told them about his visit to town for supplies.he had gone to the boomerang pub,for a counter launch,and struck up a conversation with barry humpfries the long time publican.barramaindi bill the national park ranger had come in for a few ales,and joined in the conversation.your timely arrival is most fortuitous barramundi,this gent mr wilson wants to know about the legend,of our sadly bereived friend and mate mr crusher chainsaw.i have informed mr geoff wilson,your services do not come cheap,and a consultant fee for advice on his movie has to be negotiated said barry.mr wilson you can buy me 2 beers and lunch to start,then i charge $50 an hour or we can agree on a lump sum.nothing on paper in english for the tax man to find.i will carve out a contract on a piece of bark in my lingo.you put ya monica on it job done okay.geoff wilson agreed so the deal was completed.just before he left boomerang pub,barry the publican told him barramundi,s uncle is a solicitor in darwin so the young ranger knows his stuff what.sam tilson walked into camp with a sixpack to have a chat.he listened to what was being discussed, and told them to research police records on deaths,cattle loss pets that vanished and so on.chainsaw,s both parents had been caught and made into boots and hand bags.130 traps had been set for chainsaw over the last 25 years,but he never took one single bait.he did his best to wreck every cage set up,with his 3 and half ton weight and caused thousands of dollars in damage.the cattle farmer,s near the ord river have lost 3600 head of cows or calves as the croc ranges over the whole river system.i even heard he went down the keep river and crept in at night to gobble up delilaha pure bred jersey cow.,the wyndam mayoress has a farm out there and she sent 30 men to hunt down chainsaw for a $5000 reward.salina gucci the sectertary for steven spellberg had long recorded dicussions with all wingars tourists mob.later she wrote several different short story line ideas for the movie. she showed these to maria over coffee and fresh scone .s sam tilson had given them at lunch.the 2 ladies had vivd imaginations and were creative by nature and ability.salina was an artist from a very young age and her aunt was contessa melina giogini who owned 25 fashion house shops world wide.this relationship gave her an idea,she said maria let us say 10 delicious models from many countries fly in,to stay here for a month for a film shoot.yes go on,i like the idea already said maria.so 2 contessa,s with there maids come to supervise and act as chaperon,s of course for the girls.then 4 of the girls,get lost in the bush,when they sneak away to explore.a women disappears and then the crocodilla is sighted and the big hunt is on.fantastico salina and we have micheal douglas,sean connery and 2 good aussie actors as the hunters said maria.the yank and the pom are cornered by chainsaw,and the aussie men and the local natives track them down and save there bacon.viola a master piece,a carravagio salina said and clapped her hands.that night a big barbie was laid on at wingars camp,with a full steer and a pig on the spit.many nice old recipe italian dishes were made,by the ladies only for the one night for el toro wingar the bull who charged da huge a monster and shot him dead with one bullet,to save princess dalina.the movie crew and wingars mob were sipping,wine and beer around the camp fire when salina told them about her finished screen play.maria had handed out,pads and pens to everyone to jot down any helpful ideas too.sold said wingar after he heard the full story,bloody ripper story,ill put in $10000.for a bit of the action.$50000.here said sam tilson. $500000 don tomas said and was very exited, and wrote out a cheque right then.by the end of the night 5 million was guarranteed for the movie.peter weir asked all the italian tourists to be in the movie,and they all agreed immediately.for the next 2 weeks many different scenes,filmed then a party was held at the boomerang hotel.as the crowd was enjoying a cold one,out in the back patio,they heard the sound of plane engines.chipps dundee,with his french wife glided in and landed on the dirt road behind the boomer pub,then taxied up.he stopped at the back gate.lord lipton arrived next,with dame edna everidge,in the back cockpit purple scarf trailing behind her.the pub crowd cheered them in greeting and went out back to welcome them to the party.a light plane,a cessna 172 flew over the boomer pub,and banjo from the broome bugle floated down in a parachute,he had served 3 yrs with the 82nd airborne in ww2,an old hand.the party lasted for 4 days,then wingars safari had to pack up and head for darwin.on the trip 2 of the h.j panel vans were caught in flooded roads, and had to be winched out by a unimog.a month in darwin gave the men,plenty of time to enjoy marlin fishing,and tours to local cattle stations to watch the aboriginal stockmen handle the cattle,on horse back.they saw the small chopper,s rounding up the big herds and 100s of wild camels.2 mechanics took the men,on a bore run,and were impressed with the drop down solar powered gates on the station.there was 230 of these,and it saved 100s of hours by not having to get in and out of the ute to open the gates.the ladies had massages and went shopping,then were taken to several lovely sites with there full artist kits to paint scenes.a trip to the gorge at katherine,down to aryse rock then too kalgoolie and home to perth .3 big movies were released,and all were smash hits at the box office,and grossed 25 billion over 15 years.the end of part 1-- ------------.10,30 july 4th 2015.the end. Next book title the true blue world tour by sir les hogan-patterson and dame edna rafferty take a world tour by byplane in 2016 after abbots train wreck fiasco near broome. And of course after he was hanged like ned kelly for a litany of crimes making up 4 tons of paperwork he tried to shred .bunns aviation donalds airstrip after a year of dead reckoning real barnstormer training in all conditions,and ridgid mechanical training far higher than any aircraft pilot now in the air 60% of which are uselsess in any emergency .airstrip is the take off point,then on to narromine for a tour and test flight and to deliver fresh gladiolies from dame edna,s 3000 acre nursery.donald and robert bunn flew escort with there lovely wives pranee and dolly two of the best ladies i have ever met,as co pilots all wearing the pink dame edna flying suit colours and flowing scarves sir les was trained by squadron leader norm bader in overseas flying techniques around the world,but the bunn brothers 120years combined experience set the couple up for the true blue world tour .radios were fitted to all 3 gyspy moths new engines and all fully restored.a name was painted on the side of each plane which read black watch squadron in gold leaf roberts plane was tan,a dedication to yon wee lads comedians,billy connolly the shipyard craftsman and the commando.s the ancestors of culledoon be gorra barveheart the real bloody mcoy equal to my sabre 22 squadron s,a,s the sign was 3 gypsy moths in formation a taipan in the right top corner the black watch colours at the top left corner. robert bunn flew in flying a santa fay red 6 cylinder gypsy moth too naromine, donald flew canary yellow 6 cylinder gypsy moth,alongside dame edna instructing her,to lower her speed and adjust flaps.then all 3 aircraft landed smoothly after each other.at naromine a fuel tank twice the size of the normal gypsy was fitted to sir les.s plane made of carbon fibre, special heaters were fitted and full artic flying suits,gloves boots scarves and fur lined helmets were put aboard .when increasing height the temperature drops 2 degrees every thousand feet as your altitude rises .also many of the parts were 3d printed and made of different metals.after a week long reunion and bbqs etc dame edna took the controls on her take off for darwin, as sir les sipped a hot bunns pranee thai stew from his hot flask up in the front cockpit.jesus said sir les on the radio this stew is hotter than the flamin gypsy motor, i reckon old pranee bunn dropped a lot of extra herbs and chillies in this stew dame edna,as long as it doesnt blow your socks off possum,dont want you to get cold feet it will bring on arthritis,said dame edna.sir les got on the radio and made sure fuel was ready at alice springs and darwin airports with a spot of additives,a stanby compass and a spare radio.a low profile was kept,and all call signs were sjfb22 spinfex joe the flying butcher,to keep the cusrsed media and crowds away from each landing and take off.from 1920 to 1940 many lessons can be learnt from long distance flights by the poineers of aviation smithy hinkler and the rest .the crowds caused major saftey problems and costly delays on all flights.dame edna made a perfect 3 point landing in the alice,and taxied into a hangar for a full check up refuel and overnight stay .the couple changed clothes and put name tags on mr hokey and ms credin and off they went to a private retreat 2 miles away,the sultan,s tent.four hours was the maximum limit of flight,with a few gallons of fuel, as a strict safety margin.only a complete idiot invites death trying to outfly an aircrafte capabilities with engines and fuel.sad to say,it is occuring on a weekly basis world wide now.technology and electronics have killed more pilots than any old time mechanical problems in planes from 1920 to 1950.maintenance is a deadly farce. All corrupt airlines are out to save money,not lives,there is and has never been,no safe flight in any airline in the world.wally simpson a stringer for uralula bark newspaper rang miss namjura the editor.abbots in town with the misses,i just saw em at the airport,as i chattin with dingo wallace the truckie on the shell job.hang on wally said miss namajura as she checked the latest canberra press releases.whats cooking love said wally.poor old wally your up the creek and ya lost both paddles abbot and his p.a are in newman at bhp iron ore mine for a week.bullshit i will see ya in 10minutes dingo gave me photos,i have proof. said wally.bloody hell wally,why didnt you say so,move your arse, a front page job possum.ok.sir les was sipping a tequila sunrise, as he sat on a deck chair near the pool.good gracious me we have been caught old bean with our double abbot act.the headline read assasination attempt on .pm and wife at kirrabilli house .3 robotic kelpie dog drones atacked the house setting off 3 huge bombs,of stinking fresh bullshit was scattered in a one kilometre range all around the residence.asio had set up 3 look alike couples,to take the place of the the p.m and his wife at official functions.the p.m was in fact in dubai at a conference of the oecd.bloc cs gas group lock the gate was blamed for the shocking bullshit terrorist attack.the whole media went beserk alan jones stated,we have had pure adulterated bullshit for 300years from all pollies of all parties .its overdue the prime ministers got some real bullshit in return.facebook had 2 trillion likes on the attack and a special page was set up true blue justice.by wingar hogan,pauls brother.dame edna said we must do a clive palmer and jaqui lamby act now to fly away darling,piece of piss love no worries,and we can change inta fifo miners next stop.one is most having fun as we play the scarlet pimpernal,the drongo s go charging ta newman alice dubai and every where,while we keep the bastards on the run in total despair.four police cars arrived at the nulla nulla retreat,asking for the p.m and his misses but the patterson duo had changed outfits and diguises.sir les strolled up to the front counter,and casually mentioned he saw 2 government white range rovers,with flags attached heading west to the mc donald ranges.four hancock mining vehicles were following close behind.no worries said sgt tinker,and the cops took off,back to the pub for a cold beer.wally had called them,and followed in his car to see what happened next.503 poeple were arrested as persons of interest in the attack on the dropkick p.m,including 6 ladies from the north shore quilting club.these assumed terrorists were seen,loitering with dangerous intent in front of the p.m.s house carrying large bags of possible i,e.d.s or mortars to fire bullshit cannister,s.a swat team was called in to arrest and handcuff the lot.as the arrest was,occuring 2 willys jeeps and 4 studebaker army trucks,screeched to halt.40 armed men jumped out,of the vehilces and colonel stirling aimed his browning machine gun at the swat team captian.stand your men down you stupid wanker. you have arrested lady cosgrove the governor generals wife and her 2 sisters,also lady churchill princess beatrice of holland and linda branson the billionare,s daughter who is my wife.berty simmons a royal licenced photographer had taken a movie of the whole fiasco,and was sipping a single malt whiskey,with wilbur smith the author,who lived next door, the camera still rolled as the two men,made very loud,wild and exaggerated comments about pigs dressed in uniform.berty got the world scoop and made $27000 in one day.plus t.v and story rights to a dads army like series in future.he gave wilbur smith $20000 to write a good highly outrageous story and 200 articles for the media outlets world wide.cctv camera,s had picked 4 drones flying in the sky and a blue and white,tiger moth.all these craft,were being flown from the aces airstrip on a large estate a mile away from the p.m,s house. A police chopper,landed to arrest all the pilots of said aircraft. A small man in a full biggles flying outfit and flowing white scarf, around his stolled over to the chopper.inspector howard said the whole place is locked up and your all under arrest.the small man yelled out to me chaps,we have a right bounder to deal with.then took off his leather flying to reveal a air marshall,s uniform top coat.15 men arrived all of whom were senior air force officers .all of them were ex ww2 figher aces,some retired,and others still in the airforce. what exactly are we being charged with inspector said air marshal willy strop mountbatten.a shocking terrorist attack on antonio balonio,s house the p.m no less.a hanging offence without doubt said inspector howard.your drones and a tiger moth,flew over the the official residence, at the time of the attack and we have you dead to rights.confess now and,you may get a reduced sentence otherwise you swing from a rope biggles,said the inspector.the 2 police sargeants standing near by,hokey and corman had a good belly laugh at this insult,to the air marshall.after a phone call by squadron leader james flynn 2 s.a.s army jeeps arrived and 8 men,strolled over to confront the inspector. Sgt reggie wilkons said get back in your chopper now,or my men bust a few bones,then throw you in unconscious.you dickhead copper your on secret government property without permission,no fuckin warrant disturbing men on a asio terrorist survelliance project .keep ya mouth shut about what you know and have seen .now fuck off at the double .then drew his 13 shot browning pistol and fired 4 rounds into the ground around the three cops.they bolted for the chopper,and it took off fast.always knew those 3 years at moonee ponds uni acting school would come in handy said captain peter malleon alias sgt wilkons.bloody good show,drinks on me at the clubhouse said air marshall hoskins and all the men cheered and shook hands with sgt wilkons.several other totaly innocent groups were arrested,and 4 top barristers were hired in sydney to lead class actions for $25 million damages for false arrest mental strain pstd depression etc.sir les and the misses changed into fifo miners garb and took off,for barrow creek,tennant creek and newcastle waters.on the back porch of the cattle station,a meal of bbq,d camel steaks and ceaser salad,was being enjoyed with rutherglen red wine.boomer warren drove up,in his bright yellow,toyata v8 turbo and stopped close by.he strolled over and said sir michael bronson wants a yarn with ya sir les,he will be droppin down here soon in his white black hawk chopper .he has been stayin at my place for a week,and heard about ya true blue tour mate.ten miutes later the michael bronson chopper,landed and 4 men came over.ice cold cans were handed round to the visiters and they sat down on comfortable chair,s.sir les may i introduce binty wallace ex raf,and reggie longtree ex usaf .both of these chaps are wild barnstormer,s bored stiff they told me and want a challenge before there flying days end.i have made a sponsor deal with them,and for safety sake,it would be a good idea to have 3 aircraft instead of one on your true blue tour.said sir michael bronson. myself and my good lady dame edna,shall peruse your contract in detail,old chap over breakfast and some twinnings tea,after advice from my barrister jeffery robertson,we will let you know said sir les patterson.binty said i have a spad xiii,and reggie here,this huge bloody american indian,has nuieport vii,both with new engines and just been fully restored,there in a big hangar at betaloo cattle station.reggie said we organised fuel and spare parts stops,all the way to england sir les and by the time we fly in the rest will be organised for the whole distance .binty handed dame edna the contract,and reggie handed her a large gift wrapped box.probably bloody gladiolies said sir les.not a word chaps,keep it as a surprise.said sir michael bronson.later in there room,dame edna opened the box,to find a full ww1 pilots outfit,all in fine kid goat leather,with a pink silk scarf.also a small pink pocket i pad.a station hand with a rifle,stood guard while the patterson couple,had a morning swim before breaky.there was crocs all over the place.michael and the two,pilots caught 16 good size barramundi,further down the river to be cooked later.high tea and a large,assorted breakfast was served for 2 hours from 10am.sir les,lit up a cuban cigar,and handed the co signed contract,to sir michael bronson.and said some of those,rider clauses were,below a barrister,s belt so too speak .we made appropriate changes old bean.very good a 4 million deal will,handle all the required expenses,and my staff will arrange visa,s and immigrations issues.our press dept,will look after the media.the spad binty owned was white,with fancy blue and red scroll work all over the fuselage. on each side,a peregrin falcon was painted in gold leaf,which was the mascot for binty.s spitfire 432 squadron at biggin hill,u.k during ww2.the nuieport of longtree,s was royal blue,with a 3 striped colour piece,around the nose and around the body halfway down the fusealge,the chief,s colour of the feathers on his headress,geronimo.s reggie,s apache tribe,from the hills of kentucky.four days were,taken to prepare the 3 planes,radios and equipment and specially designed, heaters were fitted for high altitude flight.binty led the flight of 3 planes as he was the most knowledgeable about flying in the northern territory.had had clocked up,six years with the flying doctor service,after fuel stops at tennent creek,larrimah,katherine and adelaide river the true blue squadron flew into darwin.10miles out from darwin a virgin airlines blimp,a channel 7 chopper and count von ricthoffen,s grandson flew out in his triple wing fokker to escort them in to land.wally dingo flynn,arrived at 300mph in his sky blue hurricane,and had too throttle right back to keep pace with the old biplane,s speed.a weeks rest was needed to organise the asian part of the world trip,next stop timor.a 20 minute press conference was held and off,the the pilots went to a private hotel by the sea.the next day 6 hours was spent,with local pilots and several ww2 fighter pilots,to gain insights from there experience in asian countries.two ex pilots from the sunderland 430 squadron,based at broome gave them invaluable advice from long range flight experinces in wartime. also the many in flight problems,that may occur,and dead reckoning navigation,without instruments and fancy electronics.these 100s of units fitted in all types of aircraft,malfunction and give false warning signals daily,causing 1000s of unnecessary deaths world wide.cheap maintenance and repairs to gain maximum profit,comes before safety and the lives of the passengers,proven since 1940 in the number of crashes and class actions in courts.on a fine Monday morning at 7 am the 3 aircraft took off for timor,sumbawa and landed in borneo,where 4000 natives were crowded around the airport.a shell fuel truck drove out to fill the planes up.then 3 willys army jeeps,and a 47 ford mecury limo drove up,and 4 people got out.the head chief of the biggest tribe and his wife,also the p.m and his misses.bangor the chief was,wearing a aussie slouch hat,with an emu feather and wore a top uniform coat,with colonels officer pips.he shook hands all round,and gave sir les a cane basket,with a shrunken head inside as an offical present.200 soldiers were formed up,as a guard of honour and carried 303 rifles in top condition,highly polished and restored .sam mangun the p.m said old bangor,here fought,with your commando,s in the jungle,and made many good mates with the men.his 2 son in laws are australians,who came back to marry 2 pretty local girls and settle down.they grow bush tucker and make,bio fuel for all the 4wdrive diesel vehicles and boats used here in borneo.the rsm a huge warrant officer,led the party,on inspection of the guard,and twenty small .native girls presented dame edna,with posies of lovely native flowers.two white holden statesman arrived to drive the guests to a large native longhut, for an official reception,with afeast of local food.a large truck arrived at the feast,to deliver fresh king prawns,barramundi,yabbies and 500 jars of vegimite.6 buskets of special seafood sauce was set down for the aussie seafood dishes.100 bunches of fresh gladiolies were,given to the native ladies,and reggie longtree,handed a box to bangor.his small son mano,opened the box for the chief.inside was a brand new slouch hat and a full iniform,and 3 carved replica models of the 3 biplanes at the airstrip now.sir les gave the p.m.s wife a gold nugget,in a big red velvet box,and dame edna gave him a top hat,gloves and a fancy cane from harrods. the feast,dancing and celebration lasted 3 days,and two more days were set aisde to rest.the true blue squadron then flew from samaninda to sabah the capital of brunei.as they banked to make,the landing approach,binty said over the radio 30 bloody elephants and six white roller,s,this bloke, the sultan must loaded lads.130billion at last count so i heard,saw it in fortune magazine,oil and gas revenue,said reggie.another week was spent in parties and visits to scenenic sights around the counrty.next on ports of call was siagon,rangoon, madrass and new dehli.the 3 planes were cruising,at 500 feet,when 7 biplanes flew up from underneath them,to form an escort ahead.a eton educated vioce,came on the radio i say damn good show,chaps .we are the kohinoor- shashin squadron gentlemen,in english and like your famous peregrin the diamond falcon squadron .follow us in,all is arranged by flying officer,blimpy branson,one of our members,ha ha.blimpy is having a massage,in our luxurious clubrooms now and getting his sprained ankle attended too.i am squadron leader omar shairrif and sad to say blimpy fell off taj mahal a young naughty elephant.there was 5 tiger moths,and 2 gypsy moths all painted a deep marone,with yellow falcon heads,on the top of each wing,and on the sides of each fuselarge.all the planes,were pushed under cover after they landed. the pilots escorted there guests to there rooms,and carried there luggage too.later at dinner,the indian couples were suprised to see curries and other dishes made of kangaroo,buffalo,dugong and goanna meat .there was 40types of aboriginal bush tucker,and lots of greens as salads.blimpy branson informed everyone taj mahal the rouge,had deliberatlcy run him into a low limbed tree,to knock him down onto the ground.he was organising the clearance of land for a solar power station he was building.blimpy also let the 3 true blue pilots know,solar panels,would be fitted to the 3 aircraft to reduce power and maintenance,and add better heating to the cockpits.a rest period of 2 weeks was decided for repairs and forward planning to karachi and quatar in saudi rabia.decisions had to be made to go to africa next,or europe then fly around africa later.sir les,binty and reggie longtree made phone,calls to different embassies.some countries in europe,were unsafe to travel in,and even more dangreous to fly over.africa was a dead loss,as any attack could occur anytime by numerous terrorist groups.a lower risk flight,was decided,with an indian air force escort,all the way,to karachi.a stop to refuel for 2 days,then off too quatar.michael,s bronson.s blimpy had alerted the tribal shieks six hours ago.as the 3 planes were,directed to a private airstrip,3000 fine bred racing camels,and 2000 arab stallions came flying in with, there riders showing there tribal flags from all,directions towards the airstrp.jesus christ who the fuck,are these blokes said binty on the radio.keep calm old chap,enjoy a glorious moment of history.remember orance .the british officer who shunned the corrupt dogs of the high command.he rode with these tribes to defeat the turks and take damascus,forget all bullshit the pompus arse generals,quote in all army reports total sefl grandizing baldertrash for a

1000 year,s sir les patterson said.who is that dude on the black,stallion,with 5 men besdie him said reggie longtree.sir les looked thru his field glasses as dame edna lined up,for a landing.bloody hell,be on your best behavior,chaps or we shall all loose our heads.i have met this shiek,he is emir yusseff abin abdullah saladin.his great grand father was the man who in 1187 gelded old richard the lion heart, and left the gay chap with a empty handbag. fuck this for a joke thought binty,and pulled,out his walther ppk,and checked the 4 grenades he had in a bag nearby .all the rider,s stopped dead at a raised hand signal from saladin.120 black tents were arranged around the desert airstrip which the pilots saw,as they landed safely.a chubby englishman arrived on a harley davidson motor bike with a side car,next to sir les as he got down from the cockpit. I say damn good show,the bloody arab chappies are over the moon,by gad,my apologies for not having a roller here,for the crew,what.said terry thomas the british consul mi5 agent.saladin and his escorts rode slowly around the aircraft to inspect them closely,then rode up,and dismounted.he walked up to the men,and shook hands,then kissed dame edan,s hand and said be at peace as one,with the desert and nature,you are my guests.all your needs will be attended too.a bentley will arrive shortly for sir les,and dame edna.binty old chap,can you ride a bloody horse.im damn sure geronimo longtree can.meet sirroco a mare,and eblis the stallion for you sir a native indian of your country,and like me a member of a tribe.the seven men mounted as 2 trucks and a bentley collected sir les and dame edna.200 arab women had come to greet dame edna,and sang and danced around the group as they drove,to the shieks large tent.there was two days rest,then four lear jets flew in with,local tribal sheiks and there entourage.meetings were held in secret and millions changed hands in bets.two days later emir saladin said too the 3 pilots we wish to enjoy great competition.a shooting contest like,they conduct in england at bisley,with the best rifles and with bow and arrows.also a falcon hunting contest on which many rhyals are gambled,if any of you,wish to place a bet dema my lady finance advisor will arrange it,is this arrangement acceptable gentlemen.no worries,and i speak for all of us,plus we play a game of heads and tails okay saladin .me old mate said binty .agreed said the emir.unbeknown to the gathered big beetin sheiks,the sly dog minister for trade chipps raferty in aussie sent in20 sets of double heads and 100 sets of the real mcoy pennies with the wooden flips.also 1dozen racing camels former champion,s at the,famous birdsville race meeting.6 indian bows 200 arrows,and 6 yew english bows and for sir les a crossbow of huon pine,and stainless steel custom made for his part in a robin hood movie at ealing studios.4 custom made wetherby rifles oiled up were in a special,crate marked urgent ladies medical supplies,via diplomatic pouch classified secret.10 2 year old peregrin falcons were flown in a seperate plane. targets were set at 500 750,1000 and 3500 yards,all 3 pilots laid down,and took there 3 shots scoring 20 to40 out of 100.the arab snipers got 60 out of 100 up to the 3500 yard targets .then all 3 pilots scored 90 to 95 out of 100.a reshoot was called at 500 yards winner take all arabs 71out of 100 pilots 97 out of 100.win.a four hour lunch break as a camel race was run nulla .nulla came first at 230 to one,and bungowannah came second at 76 to one,making 12 million for the owners of the racing camels.the sheiks immediately offered $15000 for each camel in gold bars or cash .this was agreed to on behalf of chips the minister of trade.the double,header was only used 4 times,and the arab better,s lost $600000.all up.while the aussie,s lost $200 each tops.sir les slung $20000 to the arab .bird handler to drop a touch of horse vet .sedative into the feed of saladin,s falcon,s for the big hunting safari.just at the last moment saladin,s brother amid decided to use his falcon,s who were younger and stronger.only 2 of his falcons were drugged,so the true blue pilots lost $40000 in bets.next was the archery contest,and reggie longtree split the arrows of his 4 contestants already embedded in the target at 300yards.6million cash,transfer,was made to bsb acount in gernsey island.and 12 gold bars were offered for his indian made bow and arrows.blimpy branson arranged for herbal treatment,medtitaion and massages,for the crew and 2 days rest,then the 3 planes flew to eslahan tabur and ankara.a weeks rest and on too athens. During theses flights,a special fitting had been fitted to all three aircraft,to allow a tanker to come in on top of each plane to the nozzle verticaly mounted .10 minutes for 2 fuel tanks and special lead additive .exactly the same type of petrol the day they were designed for.the landing in greece went well and full repairs and new engines were installed flown in from bunn,s aviation 116 boxwood park bungowannah new south wales.world famous areo engineer,s.at san marino airport 300 .vintage car,s and 10000 aristocrates m.ps ww1 flyers,and the twenty italian couples,who were on wingar hogan,s bush safari waited,they sipped famous aussie wines and had a bbq of seafood and bush tucker,as they waved small australian flags.the crowds went crazy,as they saw dame edna in her pink full biggles outfit climb out of the front cockpit .then she sat on the petrol tank and put on a safety belt,as sir les patterson did a circut of the airport.binty and reggie longtree,flipped there planes,upside down and flew thru,the huge empty boeing hangar,then leveled out and landed. at a runway set aside for the occasion. A bentley, 2 rolls royces and a hispano suzia drove out to meet the aircraft and the 4 pilots,when they landed.ex colonel diaz,now wore a squadron leader,s uniform as did all his mates,and got all aboard to go to a reception in a marquee close by. A caraboo transport plane landed and the back flap dropped down.two white h.j holden panel vans drove down and parked beside the maruqee.wingar hogan and sam tilson strolled in wearing white tuxedo,s and white akubra hats .heard about the true blue eyetie party colonel,so i flew in 2 presents for ya colonel .two hj panel vans fully restored a1 condition he said and handed the keys and papers to the colonel .all the italians raced outside to admire the aussie cars,and offer,s were made to buy one for $20000 pounds and more.but renni don tomsa and the rest of the bush safai crew,refused all offers,at any price. A weeks rest,tours and meetings,then off to paris,france and farnborugh airbase england .25 tiger moths and gypsy,s flew out to meet them, and escort the 3 biplanes in to land.a month in england,and the palnes were shipped home by virgin airlines .the end Thursday july 30th2015 part 3 bunger mackenzie the sperm whale whisperer.wallaby and quole,two custom made 600feet submarines cruise the world for 3 months periods at $200000 a voyage cost to the toff,s passenger.s.ex rn commander mr.bean and winston dundee a ex prawn trawler skipper are in charge of both vessels.see thru panels,on the nose and two on each side of the sub,s hull.bunger mackenzie scored $6million for each cruise,thus rollin in $12 million for both sub,s and there was a 2year waiting list on his books.there was 20 plush suits with all services provided such as herbal massage,medicine yoga,astrology kinectic therapy,vegan diet food and bush tucker from arnhem land.many passenger,s flocked to sydney from nations world wide for this exciting underwater cruise of a lifetime.commander bean in a white suit and panama hat,ushered his guests aboard wallaby,where stewards served chilled dom perignon and canapes.then a guided tour of the vessel was made,and each couple shown there quarters. A lounge and dining area was available for 12 hours only.special whale whisperer,s courses were done in the radio room,to lure the whales towards the sub for close up views by all those aboard.wallaby was powered by sea salt and electricity,and had 2 diesel engines as a back up.one hour later the 2 subs set course for new caledonia,not knowing of a french us and aussie naval exercises. salina ferago was a opera singer from vienna,and was having fun making female mating calls from the sub via special high powered microphones.wallaby was 210 miles north east of sydney at this time and within 60 miles were 24 navy vessels in all directions.piere the sonar operator aboard the french destroyer swordfish started to hear very strange sounds and furiously made adjustments to pin point the location.high pings and low drooning sounds,the ooohs and aaahs and laughter .renior the petty officer was close by and piere gave him a set of headphones and told him to listen in to the noises.what the hell is this a new chinese sub warfare technique said renior .i think that drooning sound is a baboon,like i heard in planet of the ape,s movie said piere.who is fucking laughing,are the yanks trying to create a diverson.i am getting real pissed off it sounds like a women singing.how many women crew are there on all yank vessels piere said renior .also the aussie,s could be up to no good mon ami.said piere.wallaby was cruising at 12 knots under a us aircraft carrier lincoln and dauphine a french sub was lower down going in the opposite direction.then all hell broke loose. radar,brigde 4 submarines below us within 100 metre,s said billy t wilson the operator .sonar bridge 1 possible scuba propelled vessel 1000 yards bearing 240,out. Leroy brown said. God damn you boys have been on the hooch ya all asleep at the wheel,get 4 f16,s up and 6 chopper,s drop the bouy,s find em all,take the son,s of bitches out ping em boys.said admiral ronson .mr bean was sipping earl grey tea,while snacking on watercress sanger,s and noticed a sub down below,and 6 scuba vessels pass by the viewing section of the hull,rather busy here whato reminds me of soho on a Friday,he said to jaresh the indian chef. timkins right full rudder, full ahead old boy mr bean ordered his helmsmen. pettigrew be a good chap and check a range of radio frequencies,find out what these local natives are up to bally fools are a pest he told the radio whizz.phillipe on radar in the swordfish informed the captain 8 blips were picked up,under or near uss lincoln,estimate scuba mine attack by the enemy and 2 subs id french other vessel unknown all other vessels indentified.captian hollande sent orders to dauphine to track this phantom sub down,it must be the aussie navy a ring in to confuse all ships in the exercises.commander hogan aboard peregrin,told his officer,s around the chart table,we got the yank carrier now we,hit the froggies fuck the rules,anything goes .a commando raid at night from vandetta and barracuda subs on swordfish, lyon the cruiser and the carrier la harve 3am lads when we sneak in,the wanker,s will be half asleep. leave a pet koala in the captains cabin and a wombat in the magazine of each vessel said the aussie,co.30 miles away,a swanky cocktail,dance party was in motion on the decks of both subs and a bridge platform had been slid across,so guests could go to dance at the 2 bands. The blind boys of alabama and muddy water,s blue,s band were playing as a la carte seafood bbq was cooked by 5 french chefs on the decks.winston dundee rang his mates in townsville on his satellite phone.hey t ronson how are ya,mate whats the latest said winston.had a tracker out last night,caught a bomb and filled the hull,lots going on here winno said t.ronson.any froggies or yanks around after the big marlin said winston.yep come from down south last night.in the quole,s radio room a spanish couple were trying to make there best whale sounds as whizzo topped up there tequila glasses.strange altrsound and voice messages went sent out,to entice the whales and a pod of 10 orca whales replied.all this was being recorded on tape,aboard daisy an awac plane on patrol above.well shit leftenant i been in the airforce 5 year,s,and i aint never heard anythang like this,no sir said sgt samson.i will send a copy of the tape,to the admiral and hogan the aussie .he knows these water,s better than us,them new caledoni natives might be having a looowh or somethin. Maria you make like a senorita whale,i do the el toro the bull said sancho and giggled.si sancho i purr as the kitten does,and viola the whales come yes.whizzo saw 4 orca whales come towards both subs on his t.v monitor and told maria and sancho.the awac reported 6 submarines moving slowly in the same location.commander hogan was having a scotch with bosun simmon,s as they listened to the tape from the awac us plane.bloody strange noises but how were they made commander,electronics maybe.play it again at a slower speed bosun said hogan.later he made a call to his brother professor james hogan,at queensland university ocean studies dept.james listened to the tape,and told his brother 1 minky 2 sperm whales and 4 orca.whales were having a nice old chit chat on the tape..thanks james bloody good show,and keep this confidential for the moment please okay .sure bro let me know how it turns out.said james.more phone calls to sydney followed,and half and later after lunch he informed the bosun and 2 senior officers only of the full details.the night raids on the frogs ships went off without a hitch,then commander hogan bosun simmons and 6 royal commando,s were air lifted by black hawk to the sub wallaby.commander bean was sipping french cognac in the conning tower with his russian wolfhound rufus beside him.the moon was behind a cloud and rufus gave a low rumble in his throat.a face appeared over the top of the conning tower,a navy wallah i presume just what is your game old chap rufus could take your head clean off,if i give him the word you know.said mr bean .im pissin in me pants mate,old rufus cant beat a bullet from my 45 colt old boy now lets have a civilised chat .i need some devious plans put into action that involves your 2 dinky toy subs said commander hogan.mr bean handed hogan a large pewter mug of cognac.a spot of the liore valley,s best commander said mr bean.then he informed his crew,of there new guests aboard .the two men retired to the captains plush cabin,which was fitted out with the latest secret defence and servaillance equipt as good,or not better than aboard his own ship peregrin.the comando,s were in the galley,scoffing steak sanger,s and salad while they chatted to to the chef.whats your dirty tactic,s hogan,and you must assure me there is no live ammo being used of any kind.my filthy rich passengers safety are my bread and butter..no probs,your safe just a couple of deversions while my men do there stuff.your two subs take a criuse in shallow water,s with my sub beside your,s and a mini sub with quole so the frogs and yanks give chase and get confused.4 other ships of mine will attack certain targets and we will slip away at the right time.then you head due north at full speed. here is 2 black boxes that give off genuine signals from french and american ships .divide and rattle the mind of all enemies and hit em hard,i will radio you on a certian frequency and you turn off the black boxes said hogan.ergo even a more confounding situation,and me at far greater risk a bait for a white pointer i would say.said mr bean. you will be tracked all the way and 2 awacs will keep a secure eye on your subs okay.said hogan winston and me bean were on the conning tower as a hsv 2 slowed down from 50knots to idle alongside wallaby.the bosun and 6 commando.s climbed aboard ferret the patrol boat.winston dundee handed hogan a bag and said a russian encryption machine,an advance on the old german enigma .when your opposition hear the messages,bedlam shall commence .tally ho commander said winston.hogan departed at the run and the ferret took off at high speed admiral ronson had lost his carrier,so transfered to the cruiser uss eagle to carry on the fight.0800 2 signals detected bearing 230 came the message from comm,s centre no.i.d codes suspect french manouvre of deciet encrypted .analysis shows russian nuke submarine records of the same signal type.so yesterday we had 6 subs and today we have 2 .were they all god damn whales,towed craft or decoys. said admiral ronson.sonar reports 2 vessels making for shallow water at 2o knots.there were 3 islands scattered around the excercise area,and on manus island cmdr. hogan had set up a jamming unit in an old decrepit fishing vessel.2 us destroyer.s and a french patrol boat charged in to attack wallaby and quole .as 4 shv.k aussie motor boats at long range,let go 8 torpedo.s at the us cruiser eagle.these boats had been camoflaged and hidden in the mango trees along the coast of tanoo island for 2 days.as the 2 us destroyers sailed thru a narrow channel between 2 island,s,alarms went off on the bridge,s of both ships electronic mines 2 confirmed hits targets destroyed.cmdr hogan in his sub ghecko fired 12 sam missile and took out 3 french destroyers 2 patrol boats and a supply ship,after jamming all radar radio traffic and sonar.the aussie mini sub attached mines to effiel,a heavy french cruiser .ghecko cruised in to pick up the mini sub and hogan messaged mr bean to switch off all tech units and make full speed for noumea.admiral ronson was having a bourbon with a cigar in his cabin,when he felt 5 heavy thuds on the hull.oh shit at this rate i.will end up in a bloody jolly boat for christs sake.bridge 6 hits eagle done,out of excercise all hands stand down.2 subs moving at 35knots heading due north no military i.d,maybe a russian patrol vessels.admiral roscoff one line sir said the eagle,s captain hi there old friend i have lost 8 ships,and the eagle was just hit by torpedo,said admiral ronson.mon ami those impudent wombats have destroyed 9 of my ships. A pity we could not combine forces and use madam guillotine yes,said admiral roscoff.the navy excercise finished 2 days later.a small cedar wood tender motored into noumea from the uss lincoln,and admiral ronson noticed 2 sub,s tied up at the dock.the first sub was vivid white,and on the conning tower was painted a wallaby,with sunglasses on,a panama hat.he had a vb can in his left hand and was sitting casual like in a deck chair.the other sub was royal blue with a big fat quole in a rocking chair with a cocktail glass and wearing a fedora hat. he saw a man in naval uniform,with a marone top coat and white trouser,s. sitting at the calypso bar on the shore.whose that pompus arse,in the pop eye oufit captain hanson said to the waiter.oh thats colonel t.j. bean from the english queens ghurka.regiment he is on a cruise in the white sub he said.six big well tanned men entered the bar,and sat down with the colonel .there was lots of laughing and toasts made and quiet whispered conversation then the aussie captian breton arrived and ordered a bottle of bundaberg rum.bosun harlon joined the admiral and his c.o.at there table with a new round of drinks .looks like that limey commander is cruising again he said he is a god damn colonel the waiter told us.said captain hanson. those guys are royal marines,so what are they doin here now at this time.i saw that limey on a cruiser at kuwait harbour,said bosun harlon .somethin is kinda suspect about this whole damn meeting i reckon said the admiral.when did those 2 subs arrive,have they been here for weeks said the admiral.captain hanson rang the harbour master and chatted for 5 minutes on his mobile phone.the 2 subs got into port at midnight 2 days ago said captain hanson.byron roundtree,a famous bookie from kentucky walked into the bar with cmdr hogan and after skulling a cold beer,handed captian breton a large breifcase which he opened breifly to check the contents.leroy brown saw at least $200000 grand in the brief case,as he walked by the captain and he told the bosun when he sat down at his table.also leroy informed them,he heared the group talking about ringer,s decoys and encryption and they reckon admiral ronson was like capin ayhab in the moby dick movie,a dead set old billy goat.bosun get that friend of yours in naval intelligence to this bunch of sneaky bastards right out .off the record okay said captain hanson. as the yanks left the calypso bar,they heard mr bean say loudly so barnacles ronson copped 5 good ones,up the arse bloody good show but who ran the jolly ghost submarines i say best call dick tracy whato .everyone pissed themselves laughing .captain hanson took a swing at mr bean,who moved his head away and whipped up his cane.he prodded at the captain.he pressed a switch and injected a horse sedative,that would knock the old captain out cold for a week.the royal marine,s used vicious unarmed combat methods to flatten all the yanks.a week later a secret report landed on the bosun,s desk,it stated $235000 was one by men of the aussie navy who placed bets on the outcome of navy exercise popeye in the pacific ocean,plus a lot more data.no legal evidence was found for prosecution.hogan gave $250000 to mr bean and winston onboard wallaby shook hands and wished them well .calm seas and fair winds gents .i shall let you know when any jobs arise that may need your undoubted talents he said.next day the two subs with full fuel tanks set course for auckland,new zealand.there arrival in kiwi land caused quite a stir,and 1000s of people came to see the ships at the public dock .the guests went all over the country for 2 weeks and payed guided tours of the subs were made and short cruises for the locals.off to london next with a quick stop at capetown along the way for one week only. at dock by the canary wharf london commander bean was having cocktails with contessa de guchi and her viola magazine staff.her sister marianna,had just flown in from a vacation in the pacific ocean and her boss at the australian embassy sir willy strop,had told her the aussie navy had won the navy exercise east of sydney.two tourist subs are docked at our wharf down below,you can see them thru my office window he informed her..a two hour lunch at obida italian restaurant had the sister,s giggling and smiling about the delicious rumours from the noumea gate shocking naval affair in caledonia.a series of supposed travel articles were to be featured in viola magazine.many phone calls were made and information on bunger mackenzie mr bean and mr dundee.very little was found out about bunger except he owned top hat gold mine,a sloop named 4 bob.he also had a house in the blue mountians but in his grandson,s name ballington frothesbury.the contessa called sydney and sent a chopper out to find the house.photo,s arrived by fax at her office .a huge 1000 acre property was shown with a glass dome over a underground house.there was 2 airstrips,a large workshop and 3 hangar,s for aircraft.a white 1936 daimler coupe was parked near the house and 2 camels were tied to a hitch rail.bunger tours llc was a registered company on guernsey island for tax purposes.the contessa said to mr bean capitano when did you leave ah the home port and how has your guests enjoyed the cruise so far.one has been cruising at leisure in the finest of style for 5 weeks senorita de guchi and we have 7 weeks to go.the tour may be extended if the guests want to zip thru the north pole or a jaunt to the caribee is rather popular.you may interveiw the guests if they permit said mr bean.the tug boat driver admiral ronson and his loutish oaf,s,were as drunk as skunk,s in the calypso bar .they attacked my fellow naval officers and nco.s.bad looser,s dont you know.here is the guest list,we have 4 knights,2 chinese 6italians 3 yanks 2 japanese and 3 liards from scotland .they are shopping at harrods and will attend a van morrison concert and the opera tonight.we are making video,s of all underwater marine life activity,which will be made into a full length movie later.said mr bean.where is the bungo mackenzie and what can you tell me about him,capitano.said the contessa .you can ask him,as he will arrive aboard wallaby in 15 minutes.he is touring aound in his blimp to check cruise ships along the south coast.a huey chopper landed on the pad on wallaby,s deck,and it was tied down with cables by the crew,as strong winds were building up from the north.a small jack russell dog jumped down followed by a tall man dressed in faded buckskin,s with a russian fur hat.he went strait to the forward hatch and dropped down to chat with wally benson the chief engineer.give me the news wally said bunger .a few probs with the exhaust system on the caterpiller engine,its ashore order a new 306 stainless steel unit and my crew will fit it this week without any delay,s.also it will last 3 times longer than a steel exhuast.here is a list of spares i need too.i will get whizzo on to it asap wally,now come and have a smoko with some good lookin eyetie birds bunger said .wally and bunger strolled into the cocktail bar to see winston and mr bean chatting to 6 pretty women,who were making notes and taking photos. mr bean said contessa may i introduce lord percival mackenzie,commonly known as bunger to his mates.and wally benson our engineer.it is a pleasure to meet you my lord,and you are a recluse si.said the contessa. Lets just say .i prefer the quiet life,besides i have many inventions and paintings to complete.said bunger and withdrew a a4 page document from his pocket.here is a bio,for your article in the viola magazine.sean connery is a good friend of mine,he may care to give you some of my background.mr bean is ex royal navy so his records are confidential you understand contessa guchi.the friendly group chatted more over lunch,then bunger in formed them he had a date with robert de niro at the savoy hotel and strolled off to change his outfit.wally told the girls bunger has a half share in 2 sushi cafe,s with de niro,and a opal shop in soho. salina the contessa p.a informed her they had enough datat to write an intersting article and dont forget you have an appointment at top cut diamond store in 20 minutes . dio mio grassi salina,quickly pack up and i shall,meet you back at the office said the contessa.ciao ladies perhaps dinner at the savoy some day next week,a long delicous lunch said mr bean,and gave salina his card .the italian girls departed as 6 of the crew went ashore also.all of these men were from perth w.a.and were ex sas boat sabre unit men, on there way to meet some english girls from oxford uni at the cock and hound fancy bistro bar .a supposed study on stress under harsh conditions had been funded by the psychology dept and the aussie,s were the victim,s.5 well known crim,s by scotland yard finger,s delaso beano thoms eddie the torch bazzer the knife and boom boom vader after his star war,s idol were on a job.they came into the top cut daimond shop thru the roof. beano had a real bad cough,as he smoked shit quality russian cigar,s,and had barked his shin on the shale tiles of the roof,bazzer told him to nip it as he started cursing with intense pain.finger,s handed beano,a flask and he took a sip.he nearly blacked clean out from shock.it was a mix of tequila vodka and distilled home brew 130% proof.boom boom led the way with a candle from the roof of the shop next door.a partition between the rooves had been cut away,with his mum,s garden saw,to gain entry.below were 4 arab wives and 2 sheiks,the contessa and salina and 2 japanese guests yamato and dooda, from the wallaby sub.plus 2 shop assistants serving the customer,s.boom boom whispered look for the slidin atch lad,s fuckin candle is piss poor.he said eddie the torch jumped from a roof beam to another and head butted a skylight jesus bloody hell he screamed .bazzar beat him with his granpa,s police truncheon 3 times.by now beano,had scoffed the whole,flask and was pissed as cricket.his next step saw his right foot slide off the roof beam and go striat thru the fuckin roof .grab the dumb mongrel he,s pissed,and the rest of you jump down into the store,now said boom boom vader.eddie the torch,kick more plaster from the hole in the ceiling and they all dropped down.except beano.the arab wives,screamed in shear terror,as the sheiks pulled out long curved sharp dagger,s.the first crim knocked the two arab women to the ground,and a sheik slammed his knife deep in his back before he could move.bazzar k.o.d sheik abdullah with his truncheon as he stabbed eddie.fingers delaslo landed and went strait for safe in the back of the shop and matilda an assistant drew a double barrel shotgun from a secret cabinet.she was trembling and very nervous,and pulled the trigger of one barrel and the heavy gauge bird shot embedded in boom boom,s arse as he landed on a jewel cabinet.yamoto a black belt in kenju growled like a dog and swung his right foot hard across,the top of the jewel cabinet taking boom boom legs from under him,the viola girls had rushed,into a store room,locking and barring the door.the aussie crew coming along the street had heard the shotgun blast,and rushed towards the shop entrance.finger,s had grabbed $3million worth of loose rubies emeralds and diamonds shoved them in a new briefcase he found and bolted thru the back door.

Sheik yussef suliman was in a deadly knife fight,with bazzar,when dinger wills grabbed him by the jaw from behind,twisting sharply and broke bazzar,s neck .tiny simmon,s kicked boom boom in the balls. yussef stabbed eddie the torch in the back twice,for good measure,and dinger whacked bazzar him in the throat hard.beano,had taken off to meet up with fingers and share the loot at the pigs snout tavern in soho.a police swat armoured truck arrived and 5 police cars,also 3 t,v trucks,the camera,s rolled as the shambles of the robbery was sorted out and matilda told the press $65million in stones had been stolen at least.a fire truck arrived and 5 ambulances,with siren,s blaring boom boom,s body was covered in blood,from head to toe.he had nicked 6 bottles of chilli sauce,from a supermarket 10minutes before the robbery,and they had burst open in the ensuing wild brawl to the death.the candle boom boom had he forgot to snuff out,and it started a fire in the insulation laid on the ceiling,so evryone was evactuated asap. dame standcomb ridley weilding a cat and nine tails short whip,charged into the group with her butler cantley,an ex hell,s angel bikie .she managed to flog the dead bazzer,eddie and boom boom before 3 swat team men dragged her back to her pink rolls royce parked at the kerb.frothing at the cantley said there dead men walking dame stano ill sort it here have a single malt love,calm ya nerves like,and handed her a full glass from the custom made bar in the roller.dinger and tiny rescued the viola magazine girls and took them to hospital in a metal flake blue herse winston owned to, chill his champagne before venturing on a betting trip to ascot.the arab wives went off,to a private clinic in mayfair,followed by 2 bentleys with the 2 angry sheiks aboard .these bedouin tirbesmen issued a $12 million reward for the filthy henious dogs,whom had endangered there wives and there very person.god damn,a fuckin big diamond heist $80 mill jesus said lord moncreif to robert de niro,and nearly choked on his oyster kilpatrick dish.where the hell did it happen said robert.bunger looked at his pocket map of london and said 2 door,s south of harrods old boy the top cut shop.then a video clip came on the wide screen t.v at the dorchester dining room.stone the crows,thats dinger wills,a crewman on the wallaby said bunger.oh i say jolly good,this dinger chap actually rides a damn wallaby,i would like a bet on him bunger old fruit. Robert de niro laughed like hell and said shit i will put a grand on the wallaby .it can be arranged gents,no worries.i have 30 wallabies at rabbits flat my farm in kent .lord moncrief the wallaby is in fact a 600ft sub docked at canary wharf .i have 2 subs on a tour of the world. Quite,understood i shall take a stroll down there and look up your captain he said.mr bean is the man to see me lord said bunger.the media went wild and the whole robbery story,became more exaggerated as the days passed .a boxing troop from south africa,had charged into the top shop after shots were heard,and beat the robber,s to a pulp .6 men lay dying and 4 more injured. reporters from foreign madia,could not understand aussie slang at all.in all the confusion at the top cut berty harris had grabbed 3 trays of diamond rings,and slipped them in his back pack.he gave 2 big rocks to dinger,as a engagement and wedding for salina who he was now dating,the other 3 lads had scored a few trinkets as well .the loot was kept with jock bradman a sly lawyer who worked for asio in the u.k.on certain devious tasks.fingers and beano met up with sir pettigrew napoleon lipton at his flat in palminco.sir p was a master forger and famous actor married to nicole kidman a make up artist,with her own salon marylin looks.all top quality id.s passports,visa,s etc were supplied,and nico transformed them completely .all fingers, hair was shaved off,and a brown dye rubbed into his skin.his moustache was shaved off and he looked like a bloody nigerian.nambooka fellow,s,it stated in his passport a half caste with a b.a.from oxford in sociology and fish farming.beano thoms had a beard attached and the full amish wardrobe of clobber and was now brother elisa bradon a us citizen of salt lake city utah.4 other passports issued in argentina,jamaica brazil and santo damingo allowed the 2 hoods to vanish,if the heat was turned up by local cops where they resided at any given time.the stolen stones were sold at a 25% profit to sir bennington- rice holmes,alias jeremy moncrief an agent of de beer,s diamond company,a well known fence in the london underworld.within the week a liberian freighter m.s cape palmas had taken aboard 2 passengers for a voyage to jamaica. dinger and tiny married 2 italian girls from viola magazine and bunger gave them jobs ashore in his shops.captian winston dundee was painting a seascape under a tarp rigged up,on the deck of the quole.a scene of st malo with 3 clipper,s with all sails set,and laden with smuggled cargo,racing to beat the custom patrol sloop,s.ayush the indian chef was beside him,doing yoga exercises when 6 humvee,s drove along the dock and stopped by the sub wallaby.sahib dunee pretty coloured merican jeepo.s come bugger me some more guests.maybe you drive to epsom and bust the ringer gang,willpot,s crooked caper,did not you say they wack the cobalt up the nag,s hooter yes.said ayush. no more guests booked chef,we have a full house and next Monday we are off to epsom and you will have $10000 dinaray to put a spaner in there works.i will give you the gen later,as my p.i wilson piskett is coming here today.napoleon fortitude slothsilk from the foreign office,dressed in top hat and pin stripped suit,alighted from the first bright yellow humvee and strolled aboard the sub waving his gold topped cedar cane.2 aussie security lads met him at the gang plank and asked him, who he was and what he wanted.strictly confidential old boy,hush hush and all that .lead me to your captain if you please. winston was sipping champers as napoleon arrived and filled another tall crystal glass .take a seat and enjoy some refreshment.what is your purpose here my man.said winston.i have come from the kuwait embassy captian dundee,bearing gifts and here is my card sir.at the scene,of the most diabolical robbery in british history,your chaps saved the day. at great risk,they attacked and bludgeoned to death 5 ruthless killer,s very brave lads i must say.each of the 6 security men,are to recieve a new humvee and $150000 in gold bar,s which are on the back seat of each car.the f.o.man said .he then handed a document to winston which was a letter of sincere gratitude from the arab wives and the 2 sheiks who were members of the kuwait royal family.napoleon stayed for a long lunch and ayush rushed below,to tell the aussie,s of there gifts.a mercedez arrived to pick up the f.o chap and departed. an old v12 bentley 2 seater open coupe, arrived screeching to a halt,the driver was wearing a pilots leather helmet and goggles.aah the dicko tracey man said ayush who had come back on deck with canapes and more champers.spot on chef said winston. wilson piskett a ex special branch inspector,opened a file on the table,and read out his latest report on the willpot wanker crew of nag nobbler,s.so the stewards are bribed and they drug 2 horses in each race. A small dose in one and a large dose in there winner,any issues arise the first horse is penalised correct said winston.yes now here is a list of the winner,s at epsom next Monday .piss weak laptop security these idiots have at there leeds office,a schoolboy could hack the system.you and me can win a bundle,and i want a good retirement fund in guernsy for later.said wilson aysuh and abdul will make bets for 100k,so how much can you bet wilson,

A fee off 60k is quite appropriate for servics rendered. I can raise 40k by selling some antiques,so it,s 100k each and after the race a suprise awaits. commander jenkin,s from scotland yard and professor of forensic medicine dave fleming,shall raid the stewards office,after a tip off. I will make certain our winnings are collected,before the raid .a sgt i know,will give me a call on my mobile phone.a radio call to the purser mr tibbs brought him on deck,with a sealed package of 60k in noteswhich he gave to wilson piskett.mr bean came aboard and joined them at table.we venture forth to sweden,norway,spain,the caribee then to perth and our home port sydney mr dundee. Our illustriuous guest,s put forward there votes, at lunch today from both vessel,s said mr bean.suits me to a tea and lets check nato h.q to see if there are any more exercised on our course .whato.said winston.at epsom abdul was sweating like a pig as he been to 15 bookie,s to spread bets of 50k.he had rajah and bangor with him,who were bouncer,s at the taj mahal strip club.unbeknown to poor abdul,rajah had swapped 10k of good notes for counterfeit notes,made by amit a retired printer in soho.ayush caught sight of the swap,in the far lap bar at the track and took off after abdul.he caught him just in time,before he used the bad notes and explained the problem.ayush got the bad notes and promised to fix the punk,s good and proper .keep betting and meet me at the bar later,said ayush.at the madras bistro marquee,he borrowed some oil and herbal powder,s,and raced to the bar.he asked both bouncer,s,to place $200 bets for him on the last race.as soon as they left,the bar he switched the bad notes for the 10k in rajah,s backpack.also he slipped the powder into there pints of potrgaff. abdul finished making bets and ayush used the 10k on phone bets.it was 20minutes after abdul,had returned rajah,s face turned a bluish shade and he started gagging,and moaned.that bloody madras curry i had for lunch was crook he said and ran for the loo.bangor vomited all over,the table he was sitting at and went off too.good the mongrels nearly had me jailed for years said abdul.the dogs will suffer for a week,and maybe longer said ayush. the mess was cleaned up and wilson strolled in to the bar.ok lads time to collect,and gave them each a large leather bag.back in mr bean,s cabin $634000 was shared out and mr bean informed all those present,he had made a $1million bet with bunger lord moncrief and commander jenkin,s. all the wilpot wanker,s did long prison sentences for,a list of crimes,and $2,5 million in hidden bank accounts was seized by hmg.the two subs embarked a week later,for sewden and arrived in jamaica 3months later at kingston .yamoto was strolling along the water front with mario andretti,when he noticed a fish farm named kwik catch fish and used his mono glass to take a closer look.he saw 5 men at work,and zoomed in on a dark native man with a afro haircut.mario can you go to the fish farm and take photo,s of all the worker,s please.a most impotant task yes,yamoto said what,s da game yammy,who are these dudes local mafie si that is correct mario,make like your keen on the fish and buy some.here is my cannon led camera,ok. mario did a top job and even got the workers to stand together for a group photo for a $100us dollar bribe.the two friends asked questions about who owned the fish farm,when had it opened for business and so on.yamoto told mario,about the $100million diamond heist at the top cut shop on canary wharf and the robber he saw dart out the back door.jesus holy christ 100 mill of hot stones and the robber,was a english guy right okay,so who the hell is this black hood breedin pirhana,s fuck me a,real shamozzle this is.lets go back to wallaby yammo and talk to winna dundee said mario. winston was at kingston yacht club for lunch with admiral benson r,a,n.,from the cruiser vandetta. the head waiter took them to winston,s table and seated them.after cigar,s and cognac yamoto told his story in detail .he also told them,he spent 2 years working for interpol in japan.by jove my cousin blushing betty ridley owns half of the business,i shall assist you any way i can.messages data and photo,s were sent to u.k police f,b,i and interpol.a 4 man squad was sent from special branch england to jamaica.a month long investigation found dna and finger prints belonged to one enrico carbon .he came from cuba on a visa, and now had a british passport.so fingers got away clean,and so did beano thoms .the touring submarines returned to sydney for a 3months lay up for maintenance and repairs.--monday december 14th 2015 said wee parchment done and dusted,time for a long cool pint o ale be gorra yrs james jones author 18 books so far.

Printed in the United States
By Bookmasters